Mrs. Je
Cree
Christmas

Want more Bailey School Kids?
Check these out!

#1–50

SUPER SPECIALS

#1–8

#1–10

And don't miss the . . .

HOLIDAY SPECIALS

Swamp Monsters Don't Chase Wild Turkeys
Aliens Don't Carve Jack-o'-lanterns
Mrs. Claus Doesn't Climb Telephone Poles
Leprechauns Don't Play Fetch
Ogres Don't Hunt Easter Eggs

Mrs. Jeepers' Creepy Christmas

**by Debbie Dadey
and
Marcia Thornton Jones**

illustrated by John Steven Gurney

SCHOLASTIC INC.
New York   Toronto   London   Auckland   Sydney
Mexico City   New Delhi   Hong Kong   Buenos Aires

To my wonderful friends and neighbors in Fort Collins, Colorado. Thanks for the memories.

—*DD*

To Myra Rosenfeld and her students...
happy "creepy" reading!

—*MTJ*

ISBN-13: 978-0-545-04192-8
ISBN-10: 0-545-04192-9

Text copyright © 2007 by Marcia Thornton Jones and Debra S. Dadey. All rights reserved. Published by Scholastic Inc. SCHOLASTIC, LITTLE APPLE, THE ADVENTURES OF THE BAILEY SCHOOL KIDS, and associated logos are trademarks and/or registered trademarks of Scholastic Inc.

10 9 8 7 6 5 4 3 2 1   7 8 9 10 11 12/0

Printed in the U.S.A.   40
First printing, December 2007

Book design by Alison Klapthor

Contents

1

Work, Work, Work!

"Give me that!" Howie yelled.

Eddie wadded up Howie's paper and threw it across the room. It hit Liza right on the head.

School hadn't started, but it was snowing too hard to wait outside. Kids came into the third-grade classroom stomping snow off their boots. Their teacher wasn't there yet, so nobody bothered being quiet.

"This is important," Howie said as he snatched his paper back and smoothed out the wrinkles.

"What is it, Howie?" Melody asked. "Homework?"

Howie shook his head. "It's the town's announcement for the Holiday

1

Decorating Contest," he said. All the other kids in the classroom stopped talking to listen.

"My family won last year," a girl named Carey said. "The prize was a shopping spree at the candy store. If I win this year, I'll share it with you." She batted her eyelashes and looked at Eddie. Everyone knew Carey liked Eddie.

"Well, you're not going to win this year," Eddie said. "Because I'm going to hang twice as many twinkly lights as you."

Melody looked up at the ceiling. Liza stared down at her shoes. Howie pressed his lips tightly together. His friends knew Eddie better than anyone. They also knew Eddie's grandmother. Every year Eddie bragged about decorating, and every year his grandmother pooh-poohed all his ideas.

Before Eddie could say anything more, Mrs. Jeepers entered the room. The kids

gulped. They always gulped around their teacher. After all, she was a vampire. At least, they *believed* she was a vampire. Not only that, her green brooch was magical. If they even thought about misbehaving, Mrs. Jeepers rubbed the pin and it glowed. Suddenly, everyone had to behave.

Mrs. Jeepers loomed in front of the class and flashed her green eyes in their direction. When she smiled, the kids saw her pointy eyeteeth.

"Good morning," Mrs. Jeepers said in her Transylvanian accent. "Today, I have a new assignment for you."

Eddie slid down in his chair and groaned. His teacher always thought up work, work, and more work for them to do.

"For the month of December," she continued, "we will focus on reading. You shall all read novels of your choice."

"You can't expect us to READ," Eddie blurted. "We'll be too busy decorating for the contest."

Mrs. Jeepers' eyes flashed in his direction and one long finger gently rubbed the brooch at her throat. "Everyone," she said calmly, "will read. Everyone."

"What do YOU care?" Eddie snapped without thinking. "You probably won't even have a tree."

The rest of the class gasped. Several students closed their eyes. Nobody EVER talked back to Mrs. Jeepers. Ever.

Howie tapped Eddie on the shoulder. "Be quiet," Howie warned, but Eddie was too mad to listen.

"I bet you don't even know how to decorate for the holidays," Eddie said, standing up with his hands on his hips.

Mrs. Jeepers slowly walked down the aisle. She towered over Eddie. "Is that a dare?" she asked in a quiet voice.

2

Mrs. Jeepers' Deal

The next day the kids walked past Mrs. Jeepers' house on their way to school. "I can't believe Mrs. Jeepers expects us to read," Eddie grumbled. "Doesn't she know December is the busiest month of the year?"

"I'm never too busy to read," Howie told him.

"That's because you actually LIKE to read," Eddie said.

"I like to read," Liza admitted.

"Me, too," Melody said.

"Well, I don't," Eddie said. "I'd rather build snowmen and beg for toys. Who has time to read?"

"I have time," Howie told him.

"Me, too," Melody and Liza said.

"Not for long, you won't," Eddie said, "because you'll be too busy decorating for the big contest."

As soon as he mentioned the contest, the kids started talking about their plans.

"The decorations are supposed to go with something you really like," Howie told them. "I'm trying to figure out how to make my decorations about science." Howie planned to be a doctor when he grew up. He always talked about science.

Liza wanted to make an ice castle in her front yard. "It will be like a fairy princess's Christmas," she explained.

Melody was going to make a million tiny soccer balls out of Styrofoam and hang them all over her trees. "Then I'll add twinkling blue and white lights," she said. Blue and white were the colors of her soccer team.

Eddie rolled his eyes. "Those are okay," he said. "But my decorations are going to beat the pants off yours."

Liza jumped up and down. "I just had a great idea! Instead of trying to beat one another, we could help one another!"

Eddie put his hand on top of Liza's head to stop her from hopping. "That," he said, "is the dumbest idea I ever heard. A contest is all about beating everyone else. And that's what I plan to do."

They were halfway down the block when Liza grabbed Melody's arm. Melody's mouth dropped open. Howie came to a dead stop. Eddie ran right smack-dab into him.

"What's wrong with you?" Eddie asked.

Melody pointed with a trembling finger at their teacher's house across the street.

Mrs. Jeepers lived in the old Clancy Estate. Most kids thought it was haunted. Big cracks zigzagged through the windows. Shutters hung cockeyed. The steps to the porch crumbled. But that's not what shocked them now.

Mrs. Jeepers' house glowed with twinkling lights, draping garland, and

8

dangling ornaments. Only her lights, garland, and ornaments weren't like most. Bats and spider ornaments with red eyes blinking on and off hung from the dead tree limbs. Instead of garland, white spiderwebs draped from the corners of the house. On the front door hung a giant wreath, but it wasn't made of green leaves and red flowers. This one looked like a swarm of wiggling green snakes.

"Th...tho...those are the creepiest decorations I've ever seen," Melody said.

The four friends stood there, afraid to move. That's when the front door creaked open. Mrs. Jeepers stepped onto the porch. She wore black pointy-toed boots and a long black cape lined with red velvet. She glided down the steps and across the lawn, her cape billowing in the cold wind. She stopped right in front of the kids.

Liza whimpered. Melody backed up. Howie's face turned as pale as the snow beneath his boots. Eddie looked up and up and up at his teacher.

10

Mrs. Jeepers' green eyes flashed at Eddie. One long finger gently rubbed the brooch at her throat. The green gem glowed. "As you can see, I have completed your little dare by decorating my home. Now it is YOUR turn."

"Wh . . . wha . . . what do I have to do?" Eddie stammered. He tried to be brave, but his voice trembled.

And then Mrs. Jeepers told Eddie what he had to do.

Eddie gulped and said, "It's a deal."

3

A Deal Is a Deal

At school, Mrs. Jeepers held up a green paper tree. "Everyone will get a large decoration with their name on it," she explained to the class. "For every book you read, you may design an ornament to hang on your decoration."

"But I'm Jewish," Huey told Mrs. Jeepers. "We don't have Christmas trees."

"There are many winter decorations from which to choose. Trees, candles, menorahs, stars, snowmen," Mrs. Jeepers said, showing each as she named them. "Once everyone's winter decoration has four ornaments, then we will have a holiday party."

"Hurrah!" cheered the class. Eddie yelled louder than anyone. He loved parties, especially ones with lots of candy.

"We'll be decorating for a party instead of for the contest," Carey sang out.

"And we'll be working together to win a prize for *everyone*," Liza said. She looked at Eddie with an I-told-you-so look. Eddie stuck out his tongue.

"But," Mrs. Jeepers interrupted with her hand on her green brooch. "Everyone's tree or menorah must be decorated before winter vacation in order to have our party."

All the kids in the class looked at Eddie. Eddie groaned and slumped down in his seat. "In a moment we'll go to the school library to select books. But first, let me show you some of my favorites." Mrs. Jeepers held up two books, *Champ* and *The Worst Name in Third Grade*. While his teacher described the books, Eddie sank deeper and deeper in his chair. He didn't want to read and he definitely didn't want to go to the library.

"Eddie," Melody shook Eddie's arm. "Come on, we're leaving."

Eddie shuffled along at the end of the line. Everyone else beat him to the library. By the time Eddie got to the football books, all the good ones had been taken. And the soccer ones. And the basketball ones.

"This isn't fair!" Eddie grumbled. "Everyone already got the best books. There's nothing left."

Liza held up a book about a ballerina. "Why don't you try this one?"

Eddie looked at the cover. It showed a dancer in a pink tutu. "Yuck. That's a girly book," he said with a shudder.

"Check this out," Howie said. "It tells how things work. Look, here's the inside of a computer."

Eddie looked at Howie's book. It did look interesting, but it had a lot of pages. "That's too long," Eddie said.

"You'd better get something," Melody warned Eddie. "Mrs. Jeepers is watching every move you make."

Liza nodded. "A deal is a deal. Mrs. Jeepers decorated her house and now you have to read a book."

Eddie looked up. Sure enough, Mrs. Jeepers smiled her odd little half smile at him. Eddie frowned and ducked out of sight behind the nearest tall bookcase.

Suddenly a black cloth fell over Eddie, covering his head and body. He was trapped!

4

Horror Stories

"AHHHHHHH!"

Eddie screamed and clawed at the blackness until the black cloth fell away from his face. A tall man, dressed in black from his head to his toes, except for a blood-red tie, stood before him.

"Pardon me," said the man with a thick accent. "I must have tossed my cape over your head by accident. Did I frighten you?"

Eddie stood up as his three friends came around the corner. "Being scared is for babies," Eddie said.

"Permit me to introduce myself," the man said. "I am the new library volunteer." The man bowed slightly to the four kids, showing a silver streak in his midnight black hair. Liza noticed that his

hair came to a point right over his long thin nose.

"Are you someone's grandfather?" Liza asked. Most of the other library volunteers were grandparents, and this man certainly looked very old. His skin was white and wrinkled and looked paper-thin.

"But of course. You may call me Grandpa Vamps," the man said. "Do you children need help selecting a book?"

"Not me," Liza, Howie, and Melody said together, holding up their books.

"What about you?" Grandpa Vamps asked Eddie.

"That's Eddie," Melody said, pointing to her friend. "I'm Melody. That's Liza and Howie."

Grandpa Vamps bowed again. Liza giggled and bowed back. "Eddie doesn't want to read anything," she said.

"Reading is boring," Eddie snapped. "I'd rather be decorating my yard for the big contest. That'll be way more fun than reading."

"Ah, but I disagree. Boring is NOT being able to read. I once had a marvelous collection of horror stories," Grandpa Vamps told them.

Liza shivered. She didn't like anything scary, but Eddie's eyes popped wide open when Grandpa said horror. "Now, *that* sounds interesting," Eddie said.

Grandpa looked straight into Eddie's eyes. "The stories my books tell are from ancient lands," Grandpa said. His voice was deep and rumbly, and his words seemed to hang in the air around the kids. As he talked, Grandpa waved his fingers as if he were weaving the silky threads of a spider's web.

Howie noticed that Eddie watched Grandpa's long thin fingers play through the air.

"Alas, they are locked away in a basement. My eyes are too weak to enjoy them," Grandpa Vamps said sadly. "I would do just about anything to be able to read them again."

"Anything?" Howie asked.

"Anything," Grandpa Vamps told them.

5

Tornado

"Who is ready to report on their book?" Mrs. Jeepers asked the next day at school after she'd decorated the bulletin board with a paper shape for each kid.

Howie had chosen a star. Melody had a candle. Liza picked a tree. Eddie took a snowman. He gave it fangs for teeth and two horns.

"Report?" Eddie gasped. "We have to do a REPORT?"

Mrs. Jeepers smiled her odd little half smile. "Yes. Tell us about your book. Others may find it interesting and want to read it, too."

"That'll be the day," Eddie mumbled as he slumped down in his chair. "I'd rather talk about how everyone's going to decorate their yards. I need to check out the competition!"

"I read this last night," Howie said, holding up a book about computers. He went on and on and on about the book until finally Mrs. Jeepers cleared her throat.

"Thank you, Howie," she said.

Howie beamed on his way back to his desk. Then he made a little computer ornament out of paper. He wrote the name of the book and the author on the monitor and taped it to his star.

After Howie, Carey told the class about a book she read called *Jack Frost*. She added a snowflake to her tree decoration.

More and more kids raised their hands until Eddie thought he was going to explode. "How many books did everyone read?" he shouted.

Mrs. Jeepers' eyes flashed at Eddie, but then she smiled. "A very good question," she said. Then she passed out strips of paper. "We will keep count by making a reading chain," she told them. "For each book you read, you may add a link to the chain. We'll see how long we can make it."

The rest of the class clapped. Eddie groaned.

"Cheer up," Liza told Eddie. "Our classroom is going to end up looking as festive as the neighborhood."

"But no one will decorate their yards if they're too busy reading," Eddie said. Then he sat up and grinned. "Which means MY house will be the only one decorated. I'll be sure to win! Read on, everyone! Read on!"

By the end of the week, the book chain reached all the way across the room, and everyone's paper shape was covered with book ornaments.

Everyone's, of course, except Eddie's. Melody had two ornaments. Liza had three. Howie had the most: five.

All the kids stared at Eddie. His monster-snowman didn't have a single ornament.

"If you don't read, we won't get our party," Carey warned Eddie.

Eddie sighed and went to the book-shelf in the back of the class. There were books about unicorns, fairies, presidents, scientists, and animals. There were even books about rocks, trees, and rivers.

He tried to read one, but his mind wandered. His pencil rapped on his desk. Then his feet started tapping the floor. Pretty soon he was drumming out the beat of "Rudolph the Red-Nosed Reindeer." All the other kids and even their teacher had their heads buried in a book, reading silently.

"Shhh," Liza warned, glancing toward Mrs. Jeepers as their teacher's eyes flashed in Eddie's direction.

Eddie turned a page in the book. He tried to read, but his nose was running. He got up for a tissue. He blew and blew some more. Pretty soon he was making honking noises that would scare a flock of geese all the way to the North Pole.

"Shhh," Melody warned as Mrs. Jeepers put her book down and walked toward Eddie. Her fingers touched the brooch on

her dress and then she twirled her finger around and around it.

Eddie rolled his eyes and tossed the soggy tissue into the trash. He headed for his desk. But he didn't make it.

Instead, he spun in a circle. Then another and another. Faster and faster he went until he was spinning faster than a tornado. "Help!" Eddie shouted. "I can't stop!"

"Eddie! Watch out!" Howie yelled.

But Howie was too late. Eddie tornadoed right into their teacher.

6

Living Daylights

Liza whimpered.

Melody gasped.

Howie looked like he might faint.

"I have had enough," Mrs. Jeepers said in a too-quiet voice.

The rest of the class waited to see what Mrs. Jeepers would do to Eddie.

Eddie still wobbled from all the turning. He reached out to steady himself. Unfortunately, he grabbed a stack of papers on Mrs. Jeepers' desk. Math papers. Spelling papers. Science papers. They all landed on the floor in a jumbled mess.

"I . . . I . . . I'm sorry," Eddie said. "I'll pick them up."

Mrs. Jeepers towered over Eddie. One slender finger danced over the brooch at her throat. Her green eyes flashed at Eddie. The entire class held their breath.

Would Mrs. Jeepers suck Eddie's blood? Would she zap him into a monster?

No!

Instead, she smiled her odd little half smile and pointed one daggerlike finger at the door.

"Out," she said in a voice barely above a whisper.

"Out?" Eddie repeated.

Mrs. Jeepers nodded. "Go to the library and do not come back until you have at least three books that you WILL read."

"THREE BOOKS!" Eddie yelped, but then he shut his mouth.

Howie raised his hand. "May I go, too?" he asked. "I'm finished with my book."

Melody and Liza raised their hands. "Me, too!" they both said.

When Mrs. Jeepers nodded, Howie grabbed Eddie and dragged him out the door. Liza and Melody were close on their heels.

"That was a close call," Melody told Eddie.

Liza nodded. "I thought you were vampire bait."

"I'm not afraid of a silly teacher," he huffed as the four friends reached the library. "Even if she is a vampire."

"Well, I'm scared," Howie said. "So you'd better find three books fast!"

"Wait," Liza said. "I don't think the library is open."

The four friends peeked through the window in the door. Sure enough, the library was dark and deserted. "It's unlocked," Eddie said as he pulled the door open.

Slowly, the kids walked inside. A single lamp on the desk gave off the only light. The rest of the library was shrouded in shadows. All was quiet, except for the sound of a tree branch scraping against the window.

"I wonder where the librarian is," Howie worried. "I hope she isn't sick."

"Do you think we should be in here?" Melody asked as they huddled in the center of the room.

Just then, something huge swooped out of the shadows from between two shelves of books.

"AHHHHHHHH!" screamed Liza, grabbing onto Melody.

"AHHHHHHHHH!" screamed Howie, grabbing onto Liza.

"AHHHHHHHHH!" screamed Eddie, as they all tumbled to the floor.

"Good afternoon," said Grandpa Vamps. "What may I do for you?"

"You scared the living daylights out of us," Melody said, getting up off the floor.

"I did not mean to startle you," the library helper said.

"Speaking of daylights," Eddie said, "are the lights broken?"

"I am sorry," Grandpa Vamps said. "The lights hurt my eyes. Perhaps this will

help." He turned on another small desk lamp and the four friends saw the library helper more clearly.

Just like before, he was wearing black except for the blood-red necktie. But that's not what made them gulp.

It was the blood dripping from the corners of his mouth!

7

Homework

"Did you see that blood?" Liza whimpered as the kids made their way back to the classroom.

"It wasn't blood," Eddie said. "It was grape juice."

"If you're sure that's all it was, then why did you leave so fast?" Melody asked.

Eddie shrugged. "When I told Gramps I liked scary books, he agreed the library didn't have any. So what was the point in staying?"

"The point," Howie said, "is to keep out of trouble. Vampire trouble."

But Eddie wasn't worried about his teacher and the fact he hadn't gotten any books from the library. He wasn't worried about spelling, either. Or math or science or social studies. Instead, he was worried about getting out of school and planning the decorations for his yard. He knew he was going to have to convince his grandmother to shell out some money for huge lights, sparkling garland, and giant dangling ornaments. By the time he was finished, there wouldn't be a bare spot in his yard or on his house.

"All right!" Eddie cheered when the bell rang for school to be out. He jumped out of his seat, did a little victory dance, and raced toward the door, but Mrs. Jeepers blocked his way.

"May I see your backpack?" she said with her hand held out.

"Why?" Eddie sputtered. "We don't even have any homework for once."

Mrs. Jeepers raised an eyebrow. "Oh, but you do have homework. You are supposed to read. I would like to see your new library books."

Eddie groaned and handed Mrs. Jeepers his heavy backpack. She pulled out item after item and put them on a table by the door. Paper wads. A whoopee cushion. Windup false teeth.

All the other kids in the class crowded around Eddie and Mrs. Jeepers. "Hey," Howie said. "I think those are my fake teeth from last Halloween."

"That's my whoopee cushion," Melody said. "I won it at the school carnival."

Mrs. Jeepers wasn't finished. She pulled more things out of Eddie's backpack. Paper airplanes. A wind-up mouse. Broken crayons and markers. Baseball cards. Old pieces of candy with fuzz on them. But there wasn't a single book. "We had a deal," Mrs. Jeepers said, looking at Eddie. "You are supposed to read. Where are your books?"

"I looked in the library. Everybody already checked out the good books. All that's left are boring, stupid ones," Eddie told her. "Even Gramps thinks so."

Mrs. Jeepers' eyes flashed. "So you have met the newest volunteer?"

Eddie nodded. "He's okay for an old guy. Did you know he used to read horror books? He had a whole collection before they got locked away. I wish I could read those books. I bet they wouldn't be boring."

Mrs. Jeepers smiled her odd little half smile. "I have the perfect solution," she said. "Have your grandmother bring you to my home. Tonight. After dinner."

Eddie gulped. He didn't want anyone to think he was scared, but he didn't want to go to a haunted house in the dark. "I think my grandmother is busy tonight," he said. "She's probably playing bridge, or bunko, or poker."

Liza giggled. "Your grandmother plays poker?"

Eddie nodded. "Doesn't yours?"

"I am sure she can stop by for just a minute," Mrs. Jeepers interrupted. "Would you like me to call her?"

"No," Eddie squealed. He wanted to be brave, so he stood up tall and said in his bravest voice, "I'll ask her."

"Good," Mrs. Jeepers said, putting his things back in his backpack and handing it to him. "I will see you after dinner. Be ready for a surprise. A big surprise." She smiled so Eddie could see her huge eyeteeth. They were long and pointy. Perfect vampire teeth.

Eddie couldn't help himself. He shuddered. What kind of surprise could a vampire have at her haunted house? Whatever it was, it couldn't be good.

"You're crazy," Melody told Eddie later on their walk home. "I wouldn't go to Mrs. Jeepers' house tonight for a million dollars."

They passed yard after decorated yard. There were twinkling lights and candy

canes and decorated trees. There were plastic Santas and wooden reindeer. "I'm not scared to go," Eddie lied. "It's just that I need to get started decorating. I don't have time for Mrs. Jeepers' reading nonsense."

"Thanks to you, none of us will be decorating tonight," Howie said.

"Why not?" Liza asked.

"We have to go with Eddie," Howie said. "We can't let him go alone."

"Oh, yes, we can," Melody said. "He got himself into this mess. If he had just read a book like he was supposed to, none of this would be happening."

"Don't worry about me," Eddie said. "I don't need your help." He tried to sound brave, but his voice cracked a bit. The thought of going to Mrs. Jeepers' house at night was enough to give any kid nightmares. Even Eddie.

Later that evening Eddie asked his grandmother to take him to his teacher's house. "Of course," she said. "In fact, it's perfect. I have to run a quick errand and I can pick you up on the way home."

"You mean you're going to leave me there by myself?" Eddie grabbed his stomach. The eight slices of cheese pizza he'd had for supper were suddenly churning inside.

"You'll be fine," his grandmother said, patting his hand. "I just have to pick up a gallon of milk from the store."

When Eddie's grandmother stopped her van in front of the Clancy Estate, Eddie didn't want to open the door. But he did anyway. He got out of the car and walked up to the iron gate.

Squeak.

The gate swung open and his grandmother roared away, leaving him in the dark. The only light came from a single overhead streetlight. Three black bats flew in front of the light. Mrs. Jeepers'

haunted house looked down on him like a
black cat ready to pounce on a rat.

"I'm doomed," Eddie whispered.

Eddie took three steps inside the gate.
He stopped, and at that exact moment
a three-handed creature grabbed him
from behind.

8

Spanking

Eddie screamed. That's when Melody and Liza giggled. Even Howie laughed. "We didn't mean to scare you," Howie said. "We came to help you."

Eddie yanked his arm away from his friends' hands. "I don't need your help and I wasn't scared. I was just fine until you came along and grabbed me."

Liza patted Eddie's arm. "We came here because we're your friends. And friends help one another. No matter what."

Melody shrugged her shoulders. "But if you don't want us here, we'll just go home. I didn't want to come anyway."

"Well, since you're here," Eddie said quickly. "You might as well go inside with me. You can see what the big surprise is."

"Maybe Mrs. Jeepers is going to give you a spanking for being so rotten in class," Liza suggested.

Howie shook his head. "Teachers can't spank anymore. That's something they did back in the old days when my dad went to school. He got spanked once for talking in class."

"I bet Mrs. Jeepers just wants to give him some bookmarks with names of books on them," Melody said. "That's what Mr. Cooper at the Bailey City Library does every summer to get kids to read."

"Who cares?" Eddie asked. "Let's get this over with so we can go home. I want to sketch out my plan for building the North Pole in my front yard." Eddie slapped his hand over his mouth when he realized he'd just blurted his secret.

"The North Pole!" Liza said. "That's a great idea!"

"You think so?" Eddie asked.

Melody and Howie nodded. "Your yard is going to look awesome," Howie said.

"We'll help you if you want," Melody added.

They stopped talking when they reached the end of the sidewalk. The kids walked up the creaking stairs. Liza whimpered when she got close to the wreath on the door. "It looks like real snakes," she whispered.

"They can make animated stuff look so lifelike," Howie told her, even though the snakes looked very real to him, too.

Melody jumped when a huge spider fell from a string. The creature's tongue rolled out, holding a buzzing green fly. A recording in the spider's head asked, "How about a holiday treat?"

"Gross," Liza said.

Eddie pounded on the door and it slowly creaked open. Mrs. Jeepers stared down at them. "Welcome, children. Please come in."

The children stepped inside the old house. A huge chandelier hung from the high ceiling. Cobwebs draped from the walls to the chandelier. In front of the kids, a massive staircase covered with a blood-red carpet curved up to the second floor.

Eddie leaned over to Melody and whispered. "She needs to get a vacuum cleaner."

"I think she needs a bulldozer. This place is a disaster," Melody agreed softly.

Liza didn't say anything. She was looking at a portrait of a tall man with hair as black as midnight hanging at the top of the steps. Liza shivered. It seemed as though the man in the painting was staring straight at her. "Do we know him?" Liza said.

Mrs. Jeepers paused to see what Liza was looking at. "That was my grandfather," she explained, "back in the old country. It was painted long before you were ever born."

Mrs. Jeepers turned away from the painting to face Eddie. "I have the perfect

surprise for you, Eddie," she said. "But it is down in the basement."

Melody gulped. Some time ago they had seen movers carrying a long wooden box that looked suspiciously like a coffin into the basement of the Clancy Estate. They were pretty sure that there was a vampire snoozing away inside that box. Now Mrs. Jeepers wanted them to go down where the coffin sat.

"You know," Howie said. "I think Eddie wants to read one of my books."

"No, I don't," Eddie said.

Howie jabbed Eddie in the ribs. "Oh, yes, you do. You want to read one of my books so we don't have to go to the basement. Right?"

"Oh, yeah," Eddie said. "I can't wait to read Howie's book on how a computer works."

Mrs. Jeepers grabbed Eddie's hand. "You can read Howie's book, too. Right now, I am taking you to the basement."

9

The Black Hole

Eddie could feel the bones in his teacher's hand. Her skin felt like cold plastic. When he tried to pull his hand away, Mrs. Jeepers whispered in a voice that sounded like sandpaper against rusty nails, "Hold on tight. I don't want anything . . . unpleasant . . . to happen."

With that, Mrs. Jeepers opened a door hidden beneath the stairs. The door was shorter than most and blended in with the wallpaper so that the kids didn't even know it was there. It squeaked open to reveal steps that led down into total darkness.

Eddie's face was white. Liza whimpered. Melody trembled. Howie looked ready to faint. Mrs. Jeepers pushed back thick cobwebs and flicked a switch.

Nothing happened.

Mrs. Jeepers flicked it once more.

Again, nothing happened.

Click. Click. Click. The switch sounded like knucklebones popping as Mrs. Jeepers flipped it three more times.

"Too bad," Eddie said. "The lights are out. Guess we'll all just have to go home."

Mrs. Jeepers' eyes flashed down at Eddie, but she did loosen her grip on his hand. "Wait here," she said. "I will get a light."

Mrs. Jeepers disappeared down a long hallway, leaving the four friends by themselves. "We should make a run for it," Eddie said.

"We'll get in trouble if we do," Melody said.

Howie nodded. "We'd miss recess until we're forty-two years old if we disappear from her house."

"I don't want to get in trouble," Liza said with a sniff. Whenever she got nervous her nose started to bleed. "But I don't want to go into...there." She pointed down the black hole and sniffed again.

"Whatever you do, don't let your nose bleed," Melody said, patting her friend on the shoulder. "Not when we're in the house of a vampire!"

Mrs. Jeepers appeared at the end of the hall before the kids could make a decision. She held a candle in one hand. Its flickering light cast eerie shadows on the wall. Liza, Melody, Howie, and Eddie stepped aside to give Mrs. Jeepers room to pass. Their teacher stopped at the top of the steps. Her pointy eyeteeth glowed in the candlelight. "Follow me," she said. Then their teacher disappeared down the stairs into the basement.

Howie looked at Liza. Liza looked at Melody. Melody looked at Eddie. "You have to go first," she told him, "because this is all your fault.

"Don't blame me," Eddie huffed.

Liza shook a finger in front of Eddie's nose. "If you had just checked out a couple

books about dogs or baseball or even ballerinas, we wouldn't be here!"

Eddie opened his mouth to argue, but his three friends stood with their hands on their hips. "Fine," Eddie said. "I'll go first. After all, *I'm* not afraid of anything."

Eddie started down the basement steps. His three friends followed. The wooden steps groaned with every shaky footstep. Cobwebs brushed their arms and face. "Eeek!" Liza squealed. She hated spiders more than anything. By the time they reached the bottom step, sweat dotted their foreheads even though their arms were covered with goose bumps.

Mrs. Jeepers waited for them at the bottom of the steps. "Walk this way," she said.

The basement was a maze of stacked boxes, crates, and old furniture. The candle Mrs. Jeepers held cast only a halo of light, but what they saw was enough to make their knees wobbly. Spiderwebs stretched between boxes, and black furry arachnids scurried from the light as the kids passed. Mrs. Jeepers didn't disturb any of the spiders, but Liza scratched at her neck and arms, just in case.

Melody yelped when she heard something scurrying in the dark shadows by her feet. Whatever it was sounded like it had nails. Long, sharp nails.

Mrs. Jeepers wound through the trail of boxes and spiderwebs, her feeble light sputtering in the breeze she created as she moved steadily deeper and deeper into the basement.

"Is she going where I think she's going?" Melody whispered.

She saw Eddie nod as Mrs. Jeepers turned a last corner and came to a stop. Before her was the box. The same long wooden box with brass hinges that looked like it had been dug up from a graveyard. The box they had once tried — and failed — to open.

"Is this the end?" Liza squeaked.

Mrs. Jeepers stopped and stared at the kids. When she grinned, they saw her pointy eyeteeth glistening in the candlelight.

Suddenly, a chilly draft crept through the basement. The candle flickered. It sputtered.

And then the candle went out, leaving the four kids and their vampire teacher in total blackness.

10

The Box in the Basement

Mrs. Jeepers' voice whispered through the darkness. "There is nothing to fear," she said as she struck a match to relight the candle. She gently tapped on the long wooden box with a dagger-like green-painted nail. Then one finger reached for the lid. "This is what I brought you to see," she told Eddie. "But I am glad the rest of you came along to enjoy the surprise."

"You can't open that!" Eddie yelped.

Mrs. Jeepers paused. "Why not?"

Eddie was thinking about the night he and Melody had sneaked into Mrs. Jeepers' basement, even though they knew they shouldn't. They had crept to the box and tried to open it, but the lid was locked — from the inside. Of course they had told Howie and Liza all about it. Howie had read that the most powerful vampire of all had to sleep in a box filled with dirt from his home in Transylvania. From that day on, they had all believed a bed made of dirt for Count Dracula himself was inside the box in Mrs. Jeepers' basement.

But Eddie couldn't tell his teacher the truth because then she would know what they had done. "B . . . b . . . because . . . ," he stammered.

"Because you'll break a fingernail!" Melody blurted. She elbowed Liza to play along.

"That's right!" Liza added. "You don't want to ruin that green nail polish before Christmas! It goes perfectly with your pin!"

Mrs. Jeepers smiled her odd little half smile. "My nails are strong," she said. And then she reached for the lip that ran around the top of the lid.

Snap. A hidden latch released.

Creak. The lid slowly opened.

Whoosh!

Something flew out of the box. "AHHHHHH!" the four friends screamed.

Eddie jumped back, knocking into Howie. Howie reached for Melody, who was trying to pry off Liza's fingers. They all landed in a jumbled heap on the floor. Mrs. Jeepers towered over them, the candlelight turning her face into a ghostly vision of cheekbones and pointy jaw.

"I am sorry for the dust," Mrs. Jeepers said.

"Dust?" Eddie repeated.

Mrs. Jeepers nodded. "What did you think it was?" she asked.

"Uhm, nothing," Melody lied. She couldn't tell her teacher they expected the king of all vampires to fly out of the box. That would be rude.

"Come closer," Mrs. Jeepers told the kids. "Feast your eyes on what is inside."

The kids scrambled up from the floor. Liza gripped Howie's arm. Howie grabbed onto Melody's shoulder. Melody shoved Eddie forward.

Eddie stumbled. He reached out to catch his balance.

Ooomph! Eddie fell headfirst into the box with his feet sticking straight up in the air.

"What have you done?" Howie yelled. Without thinking, he rushed forward to help his friend. That's when he saw what was in the box.

"Oh, my," Howie gasped.

"What is it?" Melody asked as she and Liza each pulled on one of Eddie's kicking legs to help him stand.

The box was full, but it wasn't filled with the dirt of Transylvania, and there wasn't a single vampire inside. Instead, it was full of books. Very old books.

"These belong to my grandfather," Mrs. Jeepers explained. "He has, shall we say, unusual taste in books, but I know for a fact that he would be very happy if you found them interesting."

Eddie, Melody, Howie, and Liza each picked up a book and looked at the titles.

"*Haunted Holiday*," Melody read.

"This one sounds good," Eddie said. "*Summer of the Ghouls.*"

"These sound too creepy," Liza said, quickly putting two books back in the box. "*Monster Manor* and *Vampire Vacation.*"

Howie read his. "*Ghost Hotel.* This might be interesting."

Liza gasped at the titles. "I don't like scary stories," she said.

Melody's hands trembled as she put back one of the books. "I'd rather read about sports," she said.

Howie backed away. "I'll stick to computer books."

But Eddie stood in front of the box. His eyes were wide as he picked up one book after another. "These are great," he said.

Mrs. Jeepers nodded. "Then you may take them," she said.

"You mean, you're going to let me borrow all of these?" Eddie asked. "For free?"

Mrs. Jeepers smiled her odd little half smile. "There is only one catch," she said.

Eddie groaned. "Not another deal," he said.

Mrs. Jeepers nodded. "You may borrow as many as you like. But be warned. These books are, shall we say, different from other books."

"Different?" Melody asked. "How?"

Mrs. Jeepers gently placed a stack of books in Eddie's hands. "They know when a person refuses to read them."

"What happens then?" Howie asked.

Mrs. Jeepers gently closed the lid to the long wooden box. "That is something you do not want to find out," she said. Then she picked up the flickering candle and headed back through the maze of boxes, crates, and spiderwebs.

11

Hideout

Carey was jumping up and down at school the next morning. "My tree is full," she cheered.

Mrs. Jeepers touched her brooch. "That is wonderful, Carey. You may sit down now."

"We are well on our way to a lovely party," Mrs. Jeepers told the class. She looked at the decorations the kids had put on the bulletin board. Many of the Christmas trees were full, as well as most of the stars and menorahs. The colorful book chain zigzagged across the room. Mrs. Jeepers paused when she came to the only bare decoration. It was Eddie's snowman.

Every kid in the class turned to glare at Eddie. They all knew if he didn't start reading there would be no holiday party for them.

"Mrs. Jeepers, everyone is staring at me. That's rude," Eddie told his teacher.

Mrs. Jeepers nodded. "All right class, let us open our math books to page 127. We have the exciting job of learning more about fractions today."

Eddie groaned. He was not in a good mood. He didn't want to learn more about fractions and he definitely didn't want to fill up his snowman with the names of books.

"What is wrong with you?" Melody whispered.

Eddie kicked his toe into his backpack. "My grandmother is so mean," he said.

"What happened?" Liza asked softly.

"She said my idea for decorating our house is too expensive," Eddie grumbled. "Then she told me to do homework instead."

Howie reached over and patted his friend on the shoulder. He knew Eddie was determined to win. He also knew his grandmother didn't like to spend money unless she absolutely had to.

"We'll help you think of something else," Liza said.

"I don't want your help," Eddie muttered. "I want to win on my own."

"Well, at least we can all win a party," Melody told him.

"But only if Eddie reads," Liza added.

Eddie sighed and looked down at his backpack. Maybe he should look at those books from Mrs. Jeepers' basement. After all, they were a little interesting. But Eddie didn't get a chance to read because he had to pass out blocks. "This is stupid," Eddie said. "Only babies play with blocks." The truth was that Eddie loved playing with blocks. He liked to build cities out of them, but he didn't want his friends to know that.

"These will help us with our fractions," Mrs. Jeepers explained to the class.

"Look at the pictures on page 127 and put your blocks on top of the pictures."

Every kid in the class did as Mrs. Jeepers told them, except Eddie.

While Mrs. Jeepers walked around helping students make different fractions, he used a long blue block and a short green block to make a catapult. Eddie whispered under his breath, "One, two, three." On three, he sent a small red block flying through the air. It soared over Howie and into the fish tank.

Eddie snickered as a fish swam out of the way of his sinking torpedo. He looked around the room to see where else he could send a block flying. The trash can caught his eye.

"Bombs away!" Eddie whispered. Another red torpedo zoomed over Howie. It was headed for the trash can when trouble struck. Her name was Carey. She walked right in front of the trash can as Eddie's block flew that way.

"Ouch!" Carey screamed. "Someone hit me!"

Immediately everyone looked at Eddie. Whenever there was trouble, Eddie was usually behind it. "It was just a tiny little block," he explained. "It's no big deal."

Carey rubbed her arm. "I think you made a bruise the size of Michigan."

Mrs. Jeepers towered over Eddie and pointed to the door. "Out," she said. "Since you have no interest in fractions, you may go to the library. Take your books with you."

Eddie reached into his backpack and grabbed his books. Slowly, he shuffled out of the classroom and down the hall. "Books, books, books. That's all Mrs. Jeepers ever talks about," Eddie said. "Well, I've had enough of that library for one week. I'll just hide out in here for a while." Eddie pulled open the storage closet and stepped inside.

In the dark he fumbled for the light switch. He felt something cold and wet, something slimy. Whatever it was, it had teeth. Big long teeth.

"Hello, Eddie," a strange voice said. "I see you have discovered my secret hideout."

"Who's there?" Eddie squeaked, still fumbling for the light.

Eddie found the switch. As the light popped on, he found himself staring right into the midnight-black eyes of the newest library volunteer, Grandpa Vamps. "What are you doing in here?" Eddie asked.

Grandpa laughed, showing his big eyeteeth. "I might ask you the same question."

"I'm hiding out from my monster teacher," Eddie grumbled.

Grandpa shielded his eyes from the lightbulb hanging over his head. "This school has monster teachers?" he asked.

Eddie shrugged. "Some of us kids think our teacher just might be a vampire."

"A vampire?" Grandpa asked. "What do you know about vampires?"

"I know enough," Eddie said. "Mrs. Jeepers is strange. She lives in a haunted house and she even has a box in her basement that looks just like a coffin. I always figured there was a vampire sleeping in there."

"Is there?" Grandpa asked, sitting on a large overturned bucket.

Eddie sighed and dropped his books on a shelf. "No, it didn't hold a vampire. It held BOOKS! A vampire would be a lot more exciting."

Grandpa laughed. "Perhaps it is one of those coffins with a secret compartment. Maybe it holds more than books."

"Cool," Eddie said with a grin.

Grandpa smiled until he looked at Eddie's books. The old man held his chest and gasped.

12

Har Har Har

Eddie didn't know what to do. Should he run for help? Should he shake the old man to try to bring him back to life? Before Eddie could decide, he heard a funny noise.

"Har, har, har," came from the old man.

"Are you choking?" Eddie asked.

"Har, har, har," Grandpa said again. "I am laughing. I was just startled to see these wonderful books."

Eddie put his hands on his hips. "You shouldn't scare people that way. I thought you were sick."

"Har, har, har," Grandpa laughed again. Then he looked at Eddie's books and stopped laughing. Instead, tears came to his eyes. The next thing Eddie knew, more tears rolled down Grandpa's face.

"What's wrong?" Eddie said.

Grandpa shook his head and began to speak in a deep, grumbly voice. Eddie couldn't keep from watching Grandpa's long skinny fingers dance in front of the books as he spoke. "I remember how much I loved those stories. Reading page after page. Stories about werewolves, ogres, and monsters. All of them like old friends to me. Now, because my eyes are weak, I cannot read them anymore."

"Well," Eddie said slowly, "I suppose I could read them to you."

Grandpa touched the blood-red tie over his heart. "You would do this for an old man?"

Eddie shrugged. "I'm not a very good reader," Eddie admitted.

"But I am a very good listener," the old man said. "Perhaps together we could make these books come alive."

Eddie gave the old man a funny look. "Books are not alive. You're starting to sound like my teacher."

Grandpa's bones creaked when he got up from the overturned mop bucket. His hands waved toward the door. "We must find a more comfortable reading spot."

"We could go to the library," Eddie said slowly, watching Grandpa's pale fingers reach for the doorknob. "Actually, that's where I'm supposed to be."

"The library it is," said Grandpa.

Grandpa and Eddie sat in the far corner of the library. Eddie opened the first book, called *Haunted Holiday,* and began to read, *"Megan ran out of her hotel."*

Eddie stopped reading. "This is a girl's book. I don't want to read a stupid girl's book."

Grandpa waved his hand toward the book. "It isn't a girl's book. Just keep reading."

Eddie groaned and read.

She wanted to see the ocean before her brother. Crash! A big wave landed at her feet. Crash! Another wave got her legs wet. "Oh, no. Mom will be mad at me for getting my clothes wet. I should have changed into my . . ."

That's all Megan said because her next words were drowned out by a huge wave. It washed over Megan and dragged her under. Only this wave didn't take Megan out to sea. It sucked her under the hotel.

Eddie stopped reading and grinned. "Cool. This doesn't sound too bad."

Grandpa nodded and waved his hand over the pages. "It was one of my favorites. Please continue."

Eddie wiggled to get comfortable on the library's sofa and started again.

Megan's brother, Tyler, ran onto the beach. His mother walked behind him at a slower pace.

"Where's Megan?" her mother called. "I thought she came out here."

"She did," Tyler said. "She must be around here somewhere. I'll check behind

that rock." Tyler jogged up the beach to look behind a huge stone that sat at the water's edge. Gentle waves lapped against the big rock. When Tyler got around to the other side, he expected to see his sister playing hide-and-seek. What he saw shocked him.

Eddie paused and laid the book in his lap. He grinned. "I like books like this."

"I thought you didn't like to read," Grandpa Vamps said.

Eddie shrugged. "This is the kind of book I like."

"Don't stop now," Grandpa said. "It's just getting to the good part."

Eddie picked up the book and found his place, but he didn't get the chance to read because Howie popped into the library. "Mrs. Jeepers said you have to come back to the classroom now. It's time for gym class," Howie told his friend.

"Do I have to?" Eddie asked. "Grandpa Vamps and I are enjoying this book. I'm reading it to him."

Howie looked at Eddie in shock. "You're reading?"

Eddie nodded. "Will you ask Mrs. Jeepers if I can miss gym?"

Howie stared at Eddie for a full minute. Eddie didn't notice. He had gone back to reading. He didn't even notice when Howie left the library with a strange look on his face.

"Where's Eddie?" Melody asked when Howie got back to the classroom. The students were already in line to go to gym.

"You'll never believe it in a zillion years," Howie told her. "Eddie wants to miss gym."

Melody and Liza gasped. Recess and gym were Eddie's favorite parts of school.

"Is he sick?" Liza asked.

Howie shook his head. "No, but something very strange is going on."

13

Fang-Tastic

On Monday, Eddie wasn't under the oak tree before school. Eddie ALWAYS met Liza, Melody, and Howie under the oak tree before school.

Howie looked at his glow-in-the-dark watch.

"Maybe he's sick," Liza said.

"But Eddie never gets sick," Howie told her.

"He could have overslept," Melody suggested.

The kids waited until the first bell rang. "If we don't go in we'll get in trouble," Liza told her friends.

Melody brushed the snow off her backpack and slipped it on. "That's just SO Eddie," she huffed. "He can get us in trouble even when he's not here!"

The kids trudged through the snow to the school. They left a wet trail down the hallway. They barely made it to the classroom before the tardy bell. When they arrived, they couldn't believe what they saw.

Eddie was sitting at his desk. That wasn't all. A huge stack of books was piled in front of him. Eddie's eyes looked sleepy, but he was smiling as he flipped through the pages of one of the books.

"You came to class EARLY?" Liza gasped.

Eddie nodded. "I couldn't wait to get here," he said in a sleepy voice.

Howie's eyes were big. Melody reached over to feel Eddie's forehead. "Are you sick? Do you have a fever?"

Eddie slapped her hand away. "I'm fine. In fact, I'm better than fine. I'm fantastic! Or should I say, FANG-tastic?"

"Does that mean Mrs. Jeepers bit you?" Liza whispered. Liza, Melody, and Howie glanced toward the front of the room at their teacher. Just because Mrs. Jeepers had never bitten anyone before didn't mean she wouldn't suck the blood of every kid in the room if she had the choice.

"No," Eddie said. "But I *have* been bitten."

"WHAT?" Howie gasped.

"Who bit you?" Melody asked.

"Not who," Eddie said. "What."

Melody poked Eddie hard in the chest. "You better explain yourself," she said. "And fast."

Eddie tapped the top book on his pile. "I have been bitten by the reading bug," he said. "I read three of these monster books. See?"

The kids looked where Eddie pointed. Sure enough, three ornaments dotted his snowman decoration. "My favorite so far is this one," he told them, holding up a book called *Fangs for the Memories*.

"You read that all by yourself?" Howie asked.

The tips of Eddie's ears turned as red as his hair. "Not exactly," he said. "Grandpa Vamps helped me. His eyes get tired easily so we took turns reading pages. I had so much fun, Mrs. Jeepers said I could go back today!"

"You WANT to go to the library?" Howie asked.

"More than anything," Eddie said.

Mrs. Jeepers did allow Eddie to go to the library. In fact, Eddie spent all of recess reading with Grandpa Vamps.

"We're going to stop by the store and buy stuff for the decorating contest," Melody said that afternoon. "Want to come?"

"We can help you find decorations your grandmother will let you buy," Liza said.

Eddie shook his head. "I'm staying after school to read with Grandpa," he told her.

"YOU? Staying after school? To read?" Howie gasped. "With Grandpa?"

Eddie shrugged. "Grandpa isn't bad. In fact, he's cool. He really likes scary stories, and he knows how to make all the monster voices."

On Tuesday, Liza suggested they all meet to start decorating their houses.

"I can't," Eddie told her. "Grandpa and I are in the middle of a chapter."

By Friday, Melody and Liza were worried.

Howie pulled his friends to the side of the room so no one could hear him. "I think we have a problem," he said. "And it's in Mrs. Jeepers' house."

"Of course we do," Melody said.

"Her name is Mrs. Jeepers," Liza added.

Howie shook his head. "No. I'm talking about those books. Remember how Mrs. Jeepers said they weren't ordinary? I think they've bewitched Eddie."

Liza gasped.

Melody sat down.

"Mrs. Jeepers did say the books know when a person refuses to read them," Howie said. "And that we wouldn't want to find out what happens if someone *doesn't* read them. The books must have some kind of magic in them."

"Don't be silly," Liza said. "Eddie's too mean to let a book hypnotize him."

Howie shook his head. "Think about it," he said. "All Eddie wants to do is read, read, read. He's forgetting everything else. Even the decorating contest."

"Howie's right!" Melody said. "What are we going to do?"

"Absolutely nothing," Liza told them.

"You mean we should let an ancient book trick Eddie?" Howie asked Liza.

"You don't know for sure it's the books," Liza said. "Besides, I think it's nice. For once, Eddie is staying out of trouble."

It was true. Eddie was so busy reading he didn't have time to throw spitballs, tie shoelaces together, or even make raspberry sounds when Carey walked by. And, by the end of the week, Eddie's snowman was full of ornaments.

Eddie stood by his snowman and puffed out his chest. "I have just as many ornaments as Howie," he bragged.

Howie gasped. He groaned. He nearly fainted. "How can that be?" he sputtered.

Howie was the best reader in the class. He always won the class reading contests. Always.

Liza patted him on the shoulder. "Don't feel bad," she told Howie. "You've probably been busy decorating for the contest. You just didn't have time to read."

"Contest?" Eddie said. "What contest?"

Melody rolled her eyes. "How could you forget the biggest event of the holiday season?" she asked.

Eddie's shoulders slumped. "I forgot all about it." He slid down the wall until he was flat on the floor. "What am I going to do?"

Just then, Grandpa Vamps knocked on the classroom door. "I have come for Eddie," he said. Eddie slowly stood up and walked toward the door. Then he disappeared down the dark halls of Bailey Elementary.

"STOP!" Howie yelled.

Everyone in his third grade froze. Even Mrs. Jeepers.

Melody gasped. Liza started to tremble as Mrs. Jeepers slowly put down a piece of chalk and faced Howie.

"Are you ill?" Mrs. Jeepers asked Howie.

Howie shook his head. "N . . . n . . . not sick," he stammered. "But this is an emergency."

Mrs. Jeepers' finger reached for her brooch. "What type of emergency?" she asked.

Melody came to her friend's rescue. "Eddie forgot his backpack!" she yelped. Sure enough, Eddie's bag was under his desk.

"We'll take it to him," Liza said. And then the three friends hurried from their classroom before Mrs. Jeepers could say a word.

Eddie and Grandpa were nearly to the library when they caught up with them. "You can't go in there," Howie said, darting between Grandpa and the door.

Grandpa's hands floated in front of Howie. "Why not?" he asked.

Howie started to step aside, but Melody took his place. "Because Eddie has a problem. A big problem."

Grandpa's hands froze in midair. "What is this problem?"

And then Liza, Melody, and Howie told Grandpa about the decorating contest. "I always wanted to win," Eddie admitted. "But now my house is the only one without decorations, and the judging is tomorrow."

"I see," Grandpa said. "You have been too busy reading to an old man to join in the holiday festivities. But perhaps I can help."

"You would help Eddie?" Howie asked.

"But of course," Grandpa said. "Isn't that what friends do?"

14

And the Winner Is . . .

The next morning Eddie stood in front of his house to admire it. His grandmother stepped outside carrying a tray with hot chocolate. "Well," she said as she passed out steaming mugs to everyone. "I never thought this would work, but you have proved to me that teamwork can succeed when all else fails."

Melody, Liza, and Howie each took a cup of hot chocolate. Grandpa Vamps stepped from the shadows of the house to accept a mug. "I work best at night," Grandpa said, "and I was more than happy to help your grandson. After all, he has helped me, too."

"We got the ideas from the books I've been reading," Eddie bragged.

"And we collected all the decorations from our attics," Howie added.

The group looked at their hard work. It was a cross between a winter wonderland and a haunted house. There was a skeleton tap-dancing on top of a Santa house, a reindeer with really big fangs, and a snow monster complete with horns sticking out of his head.

Eddie's grandmother chatted with Grandpa as the judges pulled to a stop in front of the house.

"I've never seen anything like it," one of the judges said.

"It's very clever, indeed," another one said.

"It's the creepiest Christmas ever!" a third added.

"You win!" the mayor announced. Right then and there, the mayor gave Eddie a blue ribbon and a gift certificate to the candy store.

"You did it!" Howie yelled. "You really did it!"

Eddie looked at the certificate, then he looked at Grandpa Vamps. "I didn't really do it all by myself," he admitted. "Maybe you should take this."

And then Eddie did the unthinkable. He tried to give the prize to Grandpa.

Grandpa held out his hand and waved his fingers through the air. "No, thank you," he said. "I'm on a liquid, no-candy diet."

"Then you must come in for more hot chocolate," his grandmother said.

Grandpa Vamps bowed to Eddie's grandmother. "Thank you, but I must be on my way. I have family waiting for me."

"Of course," she said.

"It was silly to think those books were hypnotizing Eddie," Liza said after Grandpa had bowed good-bye to them all and walked away.

Eddie rolled his eyes. "Are you crazy? Books can't do that. I liked reading them with Grandpa Vamps."

"But don't you think it's a little strange

that he knew the exact same stories as the ones Mrs. Jeepers had hidden in that long skinny box in her basement?" Melody asked.

Howie slapped his forehead. "You're right, Melody!" he yelled.

"I am?" Melody asked.

"Grandpa knew all about those books because those ARE his books! And that can mean only one thing. Grandpa Vamps is Mrs. Jeepers' grandfather!"

"That means there's not just one vampire in Bailey City. There are TWO!" Liza said.

"What are we going to do?" Melody asked.

"I'll tell you what we'll do," Eddie said. "Nothing, because he's one cool dude who knows how to make a really creepy Christmas and that's good enough for me!"

Haunted Puzzles
and
Spooky Activities

Creepy and Crazy Word Search

Find the words hidden in the skeletons below. Words can be horizontal, vertical, diagonal, and even backward.

Words: LIBRARY, HOLIDAY, CREEPY, TREES, SPELL, COBWEB, YARD, SANTA, SCARY, HIDE

```
L I B R A R Y
Y R A C S A P
A T H I D E E
R O R I B P E
D L L E P S R
C O B W E B C
H A T N A S I
```

Solution on page 105

Maze

See if you can find your way from the front door of Mrs. Jeepers' house to the box of books in her basement!

Solution on page 106

BUILD A MONSTER

Make Your Own Vampire Snowman!

You will need:
3 Styrofoam Balls (Note: May use
all 2" balls or 3" balls in incremental
sizes — 2", 2½", 3")
3 Toothpicks
6 or 7 Small Black Pom Poms
Black Tissue Paper
Red and Black Markers
1 Small Red Pom Pom
Glue or Paste

All these materials can be found at your
local craft store!

1. Ask a grown-up to help you cut about
a half-inch off the bottom of the largest
Styrofoam ball using a kitchen knife. This
will make a flat side to help your vampire
snowman to stand up.

2. Push a toothpick halfway into the top of the largest Styrofoam ball.

3. Push the medium-size Styrofoam ball onto the toothpick.

4. Push a toothpick a little more than halfway into the top of the medium-size Styrofoam ball. Push the smallest Styrofoam ball on top of the toothpick. This is the head. Be careful that the toothpick doesn't stick out the top!

5. Glue on small black pom poms to make the eyes and some buttons.

6. Using the black marker, draw a mouth. You can make fangs if you want! Then, using the red marker, draw some red blood on the side of the mouth (hmmm . . . or is it grape juice?).

7. With a grown-up's help, cut the tissue paper to make a cape. Try cutting a

triangular shape. You can make it as big as you want!

8. Paste the cape around the vampire snowman's neck (between the head and the body). Glue on the small red pom pom as a bow tie. Let dry.

9. Wonder what the Bailey School Kids would think of your vampire!

Graveyard Fill-ins

On pages 103 and 104 you will find a passage taken from *Mrs. Jeepers' Creepy Christmas*. But, uh-oh — some words are missing! Can you help the Bailey School Kids fill in the blanks?

Before you even look at the passage, fill in the blanks below. Try to pick words that are as silly, funny, or spooky as possible. When you are done, copy the words in order into the story. And get ready to laugh out loud! You'll have your own brand-new Bailey School Kids adventure!

1. Your name: _____

2. Name of a friend: _____

3. Name of a teacher: _____

4. Noun: _____

101

5. Adjective: _____

6. Same noun as 4: _____

7. Adjective: _____

8. Plural noun:_____

9. Same noun as 4: _____

10. Verb: _____

11. Name of a friend: _____

12. Same name of teacher as 3: _____

13. Verb ending in -ed: _____

14. Body part: _____

15. Verb ending in -ed: _____

16. Different adjective: _____

17. Color: _____

"Is she going where I think she's going?" (_____)
Your name
whispered.

She barely saw (_____) nod
Name of friend
as (_____) turned a last
Name of teacher
corner and came to a stop. Before her
was the (_____). The same long
noun
(_____) (_____) with
adjective same noun as 4
(_____) (_____) that
adjective plural noun
looked like it had been dug up from a
graveyard. The (_____) they had
same noun as 4
once tried — and failed — to (_____).
verb
"Is this the end?" (_____)
Name of friend

103

squeaked.

(_____) stopped and
<u>Same name of teacher</u>

stared at the kids. When she

(_____), they saw her pointy
<u>verb ending in -ed</u>

(_____) glistening in the
<u>body part</u>

candlelight.

Suddenly, a chilly wind crept

through the basement. The candle

flickered. It sputtered.

And then the candle (_____),
<u>verb ending in -ed</u>

leaving the four kids and their

(_____) teacher in total
<u>different adjective</u>

(_____) ness.
<u>color</u>

Word Search Solution

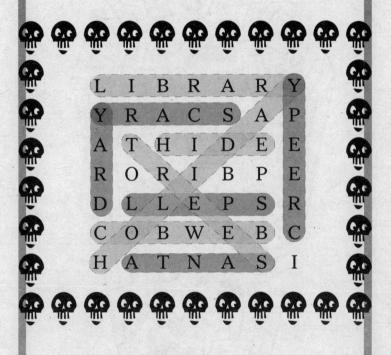

Maze Solution